A Bear for You

Written by Kirsten Hall

Illustrated by Iole Rosa

My First
READER

children's press ®

A Division of Scholastic Inc.
New York Toronto London Auckland Sydney
Mexico City New Delhi Hong Kong
Danbury, Connecticut

Library of Congress Cataloging-in-Publication Data

Hall, Kirsten.
  A bear for you / written by Kirsten Hall ; illustrated by Iole Rosa.
      p. cm. — (My first reader)
  Summary: Describes bears of all kinds, running, playing, fishing, climbing and eating.
  ISBN 0-516-24675-5 (lib. bdg.)   0-516-25112-0 (pbk.)
  [1. Bears—Fiction. 2. Stories in rhyme.] I. Rosa, Iole, ill. II. Title. III. Series.
  PZ8.3+
  [E]—dc22
                                    2004000238

Text © 2004 Nancy Hall, Inc.
Illustrations © 2004 Iole Rosa
All rights reserved.
Published in 2004 by Children's Press, an imprint of Scholastic Library Publishing.
Published simultaneously in Canada.
Printed in the United States of America.

CHILDREN'S PRESS and associated logos are trademarks and or
registered trademarks of Scholastic Library Publishing. SCHOLASTIC and
associated logos are trademarks and or registered trademarks of Scholastic Inc.

1 2 3 4 5 6 7 8 9 10 R 13 12 11 10 09 08 07 06 05 04

Note to Parents and Teachers

Once a reader can recognize and identify the 49 words used to tell this story, he or she will be able to successfully read the entire book. These 49 words are repeated throughout the story, so that young readers will be able to recognize the words easily and understand their meaning.

The 49 words used in this book are:

all	children	is	run	they
and	climb	kinds	sleep	to
are	cubs	love	sloth	too
bear	day	many	small	trees
bears	fish	not	sun	up
bees	for	of	swim	very
black	grizzly	one	tall	which
bugs	high	panda	the	white
but	honey	play	their	you
catching	hunt	polar	there	

There are many kinds of bears.

Sun bears and their cubs are small.

Panda bears are black and white.

Polar bears are very tall.

Grizzly bears love catching fish.

14

Sun bears love to sleep all day.

Polar bears love to swim.

Bear cubs love to run and play.

Sloth bears love to hunt for bugs.

Black bears love to climb up trees.

Bear cubs love to climb up high.

They love honey, but not bees!

There are bears for children, too.

29

Which bear is the one for you?

ABOUT THE AUTHOR

Kirsten Hall has lived most of her life in New York City. While she was still in high school, she published her first book for children, *Bunny, Bunny*. Since then, she has written and published more than sixty children's books. A former early education teacher, Kirsten currently works as a children's book editor. Her favorite bear, both as child and adult, is Winnie the Pooh.

ABOUT THE ILLUSTRATOR

Iola Rosa has loved drawing nature and animals since she was a child. At college, she specialized in illustration, but began her career as a graphic designer. In 2002, she entered the fanciful world of children's literature as an illustrator. Iole lives in Formello, a suburb of Rome, Italy.